the domain king
NOVELLA THREE IN THE ESCAPE SERIES

TRISHA FUENTES

The Domain King
The Escape Series - Book 3
Copyright © 2019-2024 by Trisha Fuentes
All rights reserved.

Book Cover and formatting provided by Trisha Fuentes
https://bit.ly/m/trishafuentes

No part of this book may be reproduced in any form or by any electronic or mechanical means, including information storage and retrieval systems, without written permission from the author, except for the use of brief quotations in a book review.

ISBN: 979-8-3302-0521-9 (Paperback)

Published by
Ardent Artist Books
www.ardentartistbooks.com

about ardent artist books

Ardent Artist Books was established in 2008.

We publish modern and historical romances once a month!

For a complete list of our published books and books in development, please visit our website at:

https://ardentartistbooks.com/free-downloads

FREE DOWNLOAD
Updated Monthly!

* * *

Follow us on YouTube to see what new stories are on the horizon!

https://www.youtube.com/theardentartist

Like, Subscribe & Comment

* * *

LET'S CONNECT!

Fuel your love of fiction with exclusive content and captivating insights from Ardent Artist Books. Whether you crave the thrill of modern narratives or the timeless elegance of historical fiction, our newsletter delivers a curated selection straight to your inbox.

Plus, as a welcome gift, receive a FREE downloadable eBook:

"The Family Fix"

https://mailchi.mp/567874a61a56/aab-landing-page

one

LIZ STARED at the phone for a few seconds. Turning to look at her friends first, she walked away from them so they couldn't hear their conversation on the video chat.

Turning the corner to her balcony she sat down by the edge on a bench. "Tavas?" She asked gingerly, needing confirmation.

Silence for a moment, as she watched him swing his chair around. "Yes," he finally acknowledged.

"I had no idea," Liz said, closing her eyes in disbelief.

"Neither did I," he said quickly. "You ran away before I could offer you coffee."

Liz smiled and blushed, "I had friends to meet."

"Liar," he relayed, cocking his head and shaking it.

"Well, okay...," she confessed, "I don't usually stay the night."

"Oh, you're one of *them*."

Liz grinned, "I guess I am."

"So do you make it a habit with sleeping with strangers?"

Liz was taken-back. *A personal question. Should she tell him the truth? That she did make it a habit of sleeping with strangers? How else was she supposed to have free sex with no ties? Isn't he the pot calling the kettle black? What a turn of events! Should she keep this relationship from hereon in, strictly business?* Then she thought of his nice smooth chest. "I've had my fair share, you?"

"I don't actually," he said, looking away. "I'm very particular with whom I have sex with."

Liz was very particular with whom she had sex with too. She closed her eyes and instantly brought to mind their night spent together. She doesn't even recall how they arrived at The Venetian. *A taxi, his car, did they walk?* But, she did remember making out against his hotel room door. They hadn't gone in yet when he grabbed her fierce and brought her body in. His kiss was delicious. His mouth, his breath, his tongue. Slow and gratifying, she lifted his jacket and pulled at his shirt to show her interest and invitation.

They stumbled in through the door and the hotel room was dark and cold, the only light illuminated was through the thin sections of the hotel drapery.

Liz unbuttoned her blouse, he yanked off his shirt, she unzipped his pants, he pulled down her jeans. Together, and finally naked, he pushed her body up against the dresser, spun her around until her midriff lie flush with the edges of the furniture. He took his time examining her nakedness. Fingers up the small of her back, hands touching her shoulders then back down again and around her butt. Revved up, Liz leaned over and grabbed his hands and placed them over her breasts. He immediately began to knead, massage then pinch her nipples. From behind, he entered her, a thick, full invasion.

Slowly pumping until her moans of pleasure increased and his hands gripped her hips to keep her in place. He came first, then she, yelling out her orgasm in an unfamiliar primal way.

He twirled her body around almost simultaneously and walked her over to the bed lying her down first, face up, and spread her legs wide open. Pulling off the condom, he bent down and licked the inside of her thighs and with his tongue licked the tip of her clit, then by slow degrees increased his movement to make her cry out in ecstasy for a second time.

She thought that would be the end until he rolled her over to be on top of him. She straddled his torso and felt his dick enlarge. He grabbed at her hands to make her rub him until his dick was rock hard, and ready for another condom. Rolling the latex on, she opened her legs wider and guided him in. Leaning over onto him, she slickly rode his sex when he grabbed at her neck and pulled her pucker to kiss his. Tongue on tongue, she moved her hips again, his arms and hands roaming until his lips broke free to bite at her breasts. Gently nipping at her nubs with his teeth, licking, suckling until Liz moaned out again in a sweet, salacious orgasm for the third time that night.

Liz reopened her eyes and focused on his on the phone. He was serious too, both reminiscing about their night together. Did it end there? Not by a long shot. Again on a chair until he ran the bath water in the Jacuzzi tub so they could soap each other up and have sex a few more times in the bubbly hot water.

Was it the most times she's had sex in one night?

You bet.

Was he the best she ever had?

No question.

Was it going to be difficult for her to keep their relationship strictly business?

Yes.

No.

Maybe...

two

LIZ GAZED down at the phone again then placed it to her chest. She so wanted to keep talking to him but knew it would be uncomfortable. "Tavas? I have to go, can we chat tomorrow? This..." she said, her voice cracking. "This is all a bit too much for me today."

"Yes, sure...talk tomorrow?"

He seemed wounded for some odd reason. "Tomorrow," she ended, clicking down the video chat.

Liz walked back over to her friends. If anyone could help her in her predicament it would be Cassie and Rayna. She loved her two best friends dearly and they would both have good advice.

She stood grave and dropped the cell phone to her side.

Cassie spotted the dismay in her eyes and asked first, "What's wrong?"

Rayna noticed too, "What happened?"

Liz let go a weak smile then started to pace. Pouring herself another glass of mimosa, she blurted out, "Seems as if Tavas Abbasi and I…have met before."

Cassie gazed over at Rayna first before asking, "Met before? When?"

Liz guzzled down her drink, "I met him in Vegas."

"When did you go to Vegas?" Cassie asked, crossing her legs.

"When we all did," Liz conveyed, pacing back and forth.

Rayna tilted her head, "When we got married?"

"That Vegas?" Cassie added, intrigued.

Liz stopped her stride and walked over to her balcony. She watched the surf roll over before she confessed, "I slept with him."

A hush overcame the balcony.

"In Vegas?" Cassie blurted out.

"Wait," Rayna chimed in, "you met your client in Vegas to sleep with him?"

Liz shook her head, *No*... "I didn't know it was him. I didn't know it was Tavas Abbasi until today—just now."

"Holy shit," Cassie said, in disbelief.

"Holy shit is right," Rayna exclaimed. "When did you sleep with him?"

"The night after the club," she confessed. "Well, actually, I met him at the club."

"Wow," Cassie relayed, still dumbfounded. "What are the chances of that?"

"A gazillion to one, I bet," Liz affirmed, shaking her head. "What do you think I should do? Should I continue working with him?"

Cassie and Rayna shared a look.

"I wouldn't—it would be too uncomfortable," Rayna spat out, giving her opinion.

"I would," Cassie ended up saying. "I worked with Wyatt for a while before I quit."

"You two are not helping," Liz admitted, twirling around again and gazing out to nowhere. "I need a definitive answer. Should I stay or should I go?"

"Isn't that a song?" Rayna laughed out loud.

Cassie did too, until all smiles died down.

"What's the urgency?" Rayna asked, curious.

Liz closed her eyes and Tavas immediately entered her head. Before she knew who he was she didn't give a flying fig about him, he was just work. But now...*now* that she's seen him naked, knew that his kisses were a love potion she would have rather not swallowed, she was going to find it difficult to concentrate, much less work. "Damn," she ended up saying.

"Damn, what?" Cassie asked, bringing her mimosa up to her mouth.

"I am really attracted to him," Liz confessed, realizing the awful truth.

Cassie and Rayna shared another look.

"He is rather good-looking," Rayna acknowledged, massaging her other swollen foot.

"Her type," Cassie joined in.

"He is, isn't he?" Liz agreed, turning around to face her two friends.

"And his face seems familiar for some reason," Cassie said, bewildered.

"How so?" Rayna asked, rubbing her swollen pregnant belly.

"Like I've seen him before—like on TV, or something," Cassie confessed, sipping her drink.

Liz tilted her head, "All I know is that I really like him."

Rayna and Cassie both consider their friend. Liz hadn't been interested in anyone, much less like them. It was a good sign.

"Why don't you just see what happens? Play it by ear?" Cassie asked, thinning her smile.

Liz shook her head. *She rather liked that idea. Play it by ear.* "See what he does for a change, let him take the lead?"

Cassie shook her head, so did Rayna.

"I rather like that idea, too. We women always try to take control of the situation—let's give him the steering wheel—see where the car ends up," Rayna said, wiggling her fat toes.

Cassie smiled, "Is he married?"

Liz's eyes bugged out. "Oh shit! You're right, you're both so right! What if he is married? What if I slept with a married man? What if he was in Vegas for some kind of internet domain convention and cheated on his wife?"

"What if you calm down?" Cassie let go, shaking her head. "I was just wondering if he was married, not giving you ammunition to go on a tangent."

"I know," Liz relayed, "and I thank you for that. I really do. I'm going to have to shut this down. Not ask him any personal questions, keep it strictly work...business as usual."

"Business as usual," Rayna repeated, smiling by accident.

"Strictly work," Cassie stated, smiling on purpose.

Liz grinned at her two friends and gave them the middle finger.

three

TWO MONTHS AGO, Tavas Abbasi was just a client. A nuisance, in her opinion, who micromanaged everything. Designs she wished he would leave to the professionals. Full-width images, 17pt fonts, contact forms, testimonials, now he wanted to include a bidding form that showed active bids in real time. *Ugh*...

His website turned from being a seven paged HTML to a forty page mess. He was being unreasonable. She had difficult clients in the past who wanted to dictate over her shoulder, but she had often worked closely with them and abided by their needs, but with Tavas, there was just something about him that irritated her. Maybe it was because she already thought he had a nice tone to his voice, it was only a matter of time they would meet.

Liz wasn't always this fickle. Once upon a time she was carefree and fun-loving. Her ex-husband, Aaron Tobin was to blame for this unwanted transformation.

After nineteen years of marriage, twin boys, a beautiful home in the affluent hills and money in the bank, Aaron Tobin declared he was an unhappy camper and decided to leave the marriage for solitude—not another woman or a mid-life crisis, just...*seclusion*.

Liz was convinced it was the price of fame. Aaron was a famous published author and made a fortune on his book series, a young adult fantasy that continued to bring in big bucks. He always wanted to write a follow-up to the series but never got around to it. Aaron was pleasantly happy collecting his royalties, and living alone in his Hollywood Hills home with his—*the last she counted*—four cocker spaniels.

He never was interested in being a father either, and signed full physical custody away to Liz. And once the boys were older, they never did want to reach out to visit their father and everyone lost touch.

Andrew and Aaron, Jr., (who Liz called "AJ") were both in college now. Andrew was engaged and planning to wed next year to his high school sweetheart, Carla, while AJ was happily single. AJ occasionally popped in unannounced to raid the refrigerator, stay the night or surf the waves in his mother's backyard.

Liz never did wish her ex any ill-will, her marriage should have probably ended after five years. They barely even spoke and sex was nonexistent. She didn't even weep after it was all said and done—she was just numb from trying to save it.

Aaron was still a nice guy, but eccentric. He was a loner by default, always did work better by himself and after some time, Liz figured some people were just like that. Aaron liked living a certain lifestyle, expected his household to be in perfect order, he was just one of those men who would drive everyone nuts if he wasn't in absolute silence.

Liz would have to hush up the boys with their bibs when they started to cry. Muffle their whimpers, their aches and pains, their toothaches—how could anyone live like that?

Not she.

She was glad it was all over to be honest.

She could always find someone else. She never did have an issue with attracting the opposite sex. She never needed any makeup; she was a natural beauty with long golden blonde hair, a peach-toned face, rosy complexion with deep dark brown eyes. Always a looker, she could count on keeping any man's attention, young and old.

She was also a big flirt and knew what worked and what looked ridiculous, when trying to seduce a man into her bed. And she was so relaxed with being single, she had been single for a while and like her ex-husband, she also enjoyed her solitude. Living alone, working by herself, she had no one to answer or report to. She was responsible for her own destiny—captain of her own ship, master of her own domain, *lol*.

To help her through her divorce, she had a long time affair with her old boss, Dave Edelburg. A man who had been separated from his wife. Liz and Dave had been seeing each other for the past five years. Life with Dave was never complicated. It was easy, carefree. She never gave him an ultimatum. Never demonstrated she was a woman who needed a commitment from him—*ever*—never placed any pressure on Dave at any time. So when he reconciled with his wife after five years of practically living together, it came as quite a shock. *Or maybe it wasn't*...for she knew way deep down inside that she would only have his company for a short time. She could feel so in her bones.

She lost touch with Dave; he stopped calling, stopped texting and certainly halted his coming over. She just wanted him to be happy and hoped that he *was* happy back with his wife, their kids and their home.

It did take her awhile to get over that heartache. She doesn't wish that kind of pain on anyone. That rejection, that anguish, the constant melancholy, the longing for a future that could never be.

She slept with a few men after him to help numb the agony, and that included Tavas.

Tavas Abbasi.

Hmm...

What was it about that man?

There was something different about Tavas, she had already been talking to him over the phone and through the computer, and she liked the sound of his voice. That subtle frog in his timbre, a deep gutter tone, and the way he pronounced his "R's". That sexy foreign accent, the seductive exotic way, she was bound to meet him one day, there was already too much chemistry between their verbal exchange.

Only one thing ... he lived in Colorado.

four

"IS THAT YOU AJ?"

"Mom," AJ reacted, walking over to give his mother a hug.

"When did you get in?"

"A few hours ago, used my key," he said, taking a chomp of a salami sandwich he made minutes before.

"Did you see I bought that mustard you like?"

AJ opened up his bread and showed his mother the yellow spread across the meat, "Yep."

"How long are you staying?" Liz asked, placing down her shopping bags and purse. She did a double-take when she noticed Tavas' name on her iMac.

AJ and his sandwich found their way to the couch across from her home office. "Till Saturday, is that OK?"

"Yah, sure," Liz said, fumbling through her purchases.

"Mom," AJ asked, taking another bite, "how do you know Tavas Abbasi?"

Taken-back, Liz replied, "How do *you* know I know Tavas Abbasi?"

AJ pointed to the computer. "I was surfing the net for a project and I noticed a folder with his name on it. Are you doing work for him?"

Liz smiled and was relieved for the moment, "Yah, he's a new client of mine."

"Cool," AJ relayed, crossing his legs at the ankles on a nearby ottoman. "He's really popular with the college crowd."

Liz was intrigued and stared at her son for a moment. The twins both had dusty brown hair like their father and dark eyes like hers. "Why?" She asked, taking a seat at her desk.

"He runs a podcast every Thursday night," he said, sort of matter-of-factly. "Gives students insights on how to make extra money for books, supplies and how to pay off their student loans in less than three years."

Liz raised her eyebrow. "You've listened to these podcasts? Is he any good?"

AJ perked up, "Well, he's got over 5 million followers."

Again, Liz raised her eyebrow. "Ya? Wow…are they recorded? Can I see one?"

AJ popped up and ambled over to her computer. "Here, look," he grabbed the Magic mouse and clicked on YouTube. Inside the search button, he typed in T-A-V-A and instantly generated hundreds of videos, each with dates in their titles going back several years. "He's got a podcast scheduled tomorrow if you want to view it. I'm a registered member if you want to use my login."

Liz shook her head, *Yes*. "Do you pay for membership?"

"Well, ya," he said, sort of matter-of-factly again. "$5.99 a month—it's so worth it."

Liz gazed at her computer, then said, "Thanks, AJ, that would be great."

"He's like a billionaire mom," AJ spurted out, "what are you designing for him? Hope he's paying you bank."

Liz closed her mouth, "A billionaire?"

"Ya," AJ remarked, "don't you read Forbes?"

Liz closed her eyes now. *No. No, she doesn't read Forbes. Maybe she should.*

AJ typed in "Forbes Mag" and their website popped up. He then did a search for T-A-V-A-S and Tavas Abbasi popped up. Forbes Magazine did a whole article on him.

Liz stared at his photo for a second. Shorter hair, but still just as handsome. The headlines read:

"Second Youngest Internet Billionaire"

Alarm bells went off in her head, "How old is he again?"

AJ looked at her oddly, "I dunno, I think he's around twenty-eight now."

Twenty-eight?!!

Now she's officially a Cougar...

five

A COUGAR...

That never dawned on Liz that Tavas might be married, or might be younger than she.

It never bothered her before, age. She had slept with younger men in the past, there was no difference to her, only the stamina. If she had to compare the two, she would say the only variance would be how long they could last, and how many times sex would occur. Men to her were just used for sex.

So...Tavas was younger than herself...by seventeen years?!

Oh no...maybe she really should just keep it strictly business. Would it matter? Would anyone care? Society still judged by appearance, she knew that for sure. Her age showed signs of wrinkles...why else would she work from home? The judgmental workforce was unrelenting.

Seventeen years? That was a mighty gap...

It had been four days since she heard from him. Before all this, before they knew who each other was, she would hear from him at least three times a day. That's how much of a pest he was sometimes. She guessed he was just used to people reacting immediately once he snapped his fingers. Knowing he was a *billionaire*, he probably had staff at his beck-and-call.

After checking her email for the umpteenth time, Liz walked away from her iMac and rolled her eyes, disgusted with herself. She never allowed herself to care, be so open. If Rayna was known as the *Ice Queen*, Liz was known as the *Devil in Disguise*. She could cut you off without an explanation. She would never collect phone numbers after a hookup on a dating app, she just wouldn't give a damn. Maybe she was a little selfish, but she couldn't care less...*now she did*.

She cared too much that Tavas Abbasi wasn't kissing her feet like other men in her past would. Maybe that was the real problem?

Tavas Abbasi was officially a challenge.

Yea for challenges!

Could the Cougar trap her young prey?

She was definitely up for the task.

Yea for tasks!

She was just about to sit on the balcony with her laptop, when her doorbell rang. She didn't think much of it, it wasn't Saturday yet and AJ was still at home.

She thought her son would get the door when the doorbell rang, again.

"AJ?" Liz called out towards the great room.

"I got it!" AJ yelled back towards her area.

Liz put her feet up on the other end of the outdoor couch and made herself comfortable. She lifted the face of her laptop when in the corner of her eye she sees her son with his guest appear.

"You expecting someone mom?" AJ asked, grinning ear to ear.

Liz turned her head and received the second shock of her life. *Tavas?!* "Oh hell...," she let go by mistake.

Tavas smiled, "Nice to see you too."

Liz sat up and then swung her feet back down to the deck. "What are you doing here? How did you know where I lived?"

Tavas took off his aviator glasses then turned to look at AJ first, "I have my ways."

AJ grinned again, and then declared, "I'm gonna head out for a while."

"Where you going?" Liz asked, all motherly like.

"Some of my friends are going to this bar in town, I'm gonna meet them there," he said, exiting the twosome and the awkwardness of the conversation.

Liz smiled at Tavas and then watched her son shake hands with him.

"Nice to meet you Tavas, love the podcasts," AJ quipped, patting Tavas on his shoulder.

"Nice to meet you as well. Write your registration number down so I can have my assistant issue you a lifetime pass," Tavas let go, graciously.

AJ waved goodbye and Liz watched her son leave around the corner.

She then stood up and walked over to her unannounced house guest. Closed mouthed, she eyed him standing there, incredulous that he was now in her home. *Damn, he was handsome in the sunlight.* Dark brown, almost black wavy hair cut long around his neck. Dark heavenly eyes and that sexy mouth of his. She dropped her eyes to his attire. He was dressed business casual, like he had just come from a meeting. She was glad to see him though. Her heart pounding abruptly told her that. "How are you?"

Tavas grinned then walked past her towards the balcony's edge. Admiring her glorious sea cliff view and the waves below, he turned around and asked, "This is your house?"

Liz cocked her head, "Yes, why?"

"When I had my assistant research your address, I thought I was coming to see you at your office, not your home."

Liz bit down on her lower lip, "Yea, I could see how you could mix that up. As you can see, I work from home."

Tavas smiled and then gazed out towards the sunset. "It's beautiful here...what is this, Malibu?"

Liz shook her head, "Yes. I've been here for about twenty years now."

Tavas lowered his eyes to her simple T-shirt and gym pants, then gazed down at her bare feet. "Were you heading down to the beach? Was I interrupting anything?"

Liz eyed her bare toes, she never did wear shoes around her house. *Why did she need to?* She would occasionally wear flip flops, but even those were scarce. "I was about to Photoshop some artwork I received from another client of mine, but that can wait." She then noted his strange behavior. Something was on his mind. "What's going on? Why did you come all this way?"

"I wanted to see you in person," he said quickly, circling his eyes around her face.

Liz' heart dropped. She had forgotten to *put on her face*. She wasn't expecting any company—it was just a normal work day for her. "You want to go over some of the new development updates I deployed the other day? You can see my home office," she joked, dropping her eyes to his mouth by accident.

Tavas dropped his eyes towards hers as well. "It's nice to see you again."

Liz grinned into his sensuality. "It's nice to see you as well. I was wondering when I was going to hear from you."

Tavas enclosed the space between them. "I've thought a lot about you."

"How so?" Liz whispered.

Tavas leaned over and grabbed her by her waist, drawing her body into his. Liz was a most willing participant. "I miss touching you."

six

BARELY A FEW INCHES away from his face, Liz could view him in a clearer light. In Vegas, their encounter was in the dark and she could barely fit the pieces together. With the sunset on her balcony, his facade was a gorgeous exotic masculine masterpiece. "Are you married?"

Tavas blinked back his surprise. "No, why?"

Liz let go a wide smile then kissed him softly on the lips, "I missed touching you too."

Tavas' warm hands wrapped around her waist.

Liz no longer wanted to cheat herself and released all her inhibitions. She was so drawn to him, she allowed the reality of his presence in her home, by her side, chest abutting his. He travelled to see her, inquired about her location, hopped on a plane, and scheduled some actual time in his calendar to wrap his arms around her.

That was a *win* in her book.

Liz leaned in and tested his indecision—and, as she anticipated—he had none. Her kiss was met with an open mouthed prize. His tongue in her mouth, the taste of him, hot and wet, melted her resolve.

Making out on the balcony turned heated and frenzied, and Liz quickly broke apart from him and grabbed at his hand. In a low tone, she softly asked, "Should we take this to my room?"

With fervent eyes, Tavas looked down at her mouth, "Is anyone else here?"

Liz gave him a peck on his lips, "No, just me."

Tavas then pulled at her arm, "Let's hurry then."

Liz smiled, then walked with him fast through the great room, her home office, then down the staircase and into her bedroom. Locking the door behind her she hesitated with her back against the door. "You've come a long way, would you like to take a shower?"

Tavas walked over to her private balcony that overlooked the ocean. He let go a sensuous grin, "You've read my mind. Will you wash my back?"

Liz pulled her shirt up over her head. Standing there in her bra and spandex, she voiced, "Meet you in the bathroom?"

Tavas began to walk backwards as he disrobed. First his jacket, then unbuttoning his shirt, he pulled it out from within his jeans. Slipping off his shoes, he met her gaze and they came together in a passionate embrace.

Liz walked him over to the shower and stood in front of him as she aided Tavas unroll his socks and drew down his pants and underwear. Dropping her eyes down to the small tuft of hair that framed his erect penis, Liz unclipped her bra and then tossed it out towards her vanity.

Turning the knobs to the water, Liz guided him into her large walk-in shower and under her rainfall showerhead. She wrapped her arms around his neck, and began kissing his wet mouth as he dipped their heads under the hot water. Slicking her hair back, she grabbed the soft soap and squirted the substance onto the palms of her hands and began to lather his body up with the white cream. First his back, over his shoulders, down to his waist and then around to the front of his body where she ran her hands up his chest then down towards his groin.

From behind, her soapy hands slicked his penis, up and down, then slowly up and back until she could hear his moans coming deep down within his throat.

"My turn," Tavas voiced, twisting her body around and grabbing the soft soap. He was just about to pour the soap on her back when he looked up in the corner of the shower. There was a handle bar in the ceiling by the edge of the shower? He laughed out loud, "Is that what I think it is?"

Liz didn't even have to look up and turned around to face him. Running her head under the rainfall first, she slicked back her own head of hair and backed up towards the handle. Raising her hands in the air, she grabbed the handle bars and lifted herself up. "Giddy up."

Tavas smiled then walked in towards her. Like a man who just discovered a new way to scratch himself, Tavas lifted her hips up so Liz' legs could wrap around his waist. Not entering her yet, his mouth found her breasts and he took his time on each one of them. Licking, suckling and massaging both, while Liz threw her head back and moaned out in pleasure hanging on the handle bars.

The sexual position being so convenient, Tavas pressed into her and back out again and guided his manhood in and out as he watched the carnal motion. Her legs squeezed, her back arched, and his pleasure only intensified.

Tavas pumped a few times and threw his head back in ultimate orgasm. Liz too, yelled out loud and wiggled and jerked around him.

Breathing heavily, Tavas gently released her arms from the handle bar and kissed each breast before setting her down. Walking over to run his body under the rainfall shower, he closed his eyes and allowed the hot drizzle to cleanse his face and run down his naked body. Reopening his eyes he gazed down at Liz who repositioned herself and stood face to face. "Would you mind if I took a nap?"

Liz leaned in and kissed his neck, "You're tired?"

"Yea," he said truthfully, "I just landed from a 14-hour flight from Dubai. I was visiting my mother on holiday."

seven

LIZ SAT BACK on a loveseat in the corner of her bedroom, and silently watched Tavas sleeping soundly in her bed.

It had been six hours since their shower, and she had sat silently and sipped her coffee while trying to size him up.

He was a most curious specimen, so driven for someone under thirty. Never married — *she did Google that* — and graduated from Harvard with a master's in business. He was born in Elahieh, an affluent and upper-class district in Northern Tehran. His father was murdered during a bombing protest in the ninetie,s and his mother was born from royal blood? *Why hadn't she heard of him before? This podcast guru — this domain king?*

He would be her technical match. He was self-made, and so was she. Liz was already making six figures on her own. She had been self-sufficient for years now, Aaron paid for the twins' college tuition, their room and board, Liz never had to worry about money for the boys.

She had already set aside some of her savings to help pay for Andrew's wedding next year, she even offered to chip in for their honeymoon. Between Cassie, Rayna and Liz, it was Liz who held the most wealth. She wasn't born into it, she earned every penny of her fortune.

Yes, it was true, she wouldn't normally shave her armpits or shave her legs...why would she need to? Her best friends would often tease her about it, but they still loved her...she was just, different.

But she was body conscious and hired a personal trainer to come to her home, and dedicated a room in her house for a personal gym with weights, floor length mirrors and rubber mats. Not believing in liposuction either, breast augmentation, botox, cosmetic or plastic surgery, Liz committed herself to herbal facials weekly, and a nutritionist to make sure she was eating right.

When Cassie got her breast implants, Liz did contemplate and play with the idea of increasing her B to a C cup, but her natural breasts held up after breast-feeding twins and her trainer helped her to work on the muscle behind the chest to naturally lift them up. And besides, Liz never received any complaints from any of the men she slept with, not even Tavas, who seemed especially absorbed in her two small mounds, and rather liked her braless for easier access.

She *really* liked him. More so now that she knew he held a brain behind all that tanned skin. It turned her on even more.

His black hair was long around his face but cut around his ears and neck. Every inch of him exuded sex appeal and she figured 95% of his 5 million followers on YouTube must have been female.

She was beginning to hold deep feelings for him, she realized immediately, watching him sleeping soundly between her covers. She allowed him access into her bedroom, sleep in her bed, and privy into her private life.

He was so mysterious and openly public at the same time. A contradiction of sorts; a man whom she would have never met if not for his interest in developing a website.

Speaking of his website, funny how sex could melt away all those previous frustrations she held for him. Now, all she wanted to do was help him, take care of him, feed his hunger any way she could think of.

Tavas stirred in his sleep a few times, mumbled a few incoherent words. She thought she heard the word *No* and *that's not what I wanted.*

Having so much responsibility she assumed he must be under so much pressure; preparing for his Thursday podcasts, marketing his ideas, building up his social media, creating and designing his business website. Another venture; more money in the bank. Curious, he never did mention including a page for his podcast videos. *Should she ask him when he woke up?*

He tossed again — which caused Liz to look up from her staring out in space.

His family on his mother's side, came from royal blood. *What did that mean exactly? Was he a secret prince? Did his family hold riches in Tehran? Oil or land?* She would have to ask him when he woke up.

He flipped his leg across the bed to expose a well-defined honey-toned leg. It reminded her of the morning when she left him in the hotel room. It was a magical night. An interlude of awareness…maybe it was fate?

She remembered the thrill of seeing him for the first time at the roulette table with those aviator glasses, trying to focus on the chips on the table when in fact, he was looking at her.

That little thought made her smile, until she heard Tavas murmuring again. Moaning something inaudible, she pepped up when she finally did hear something discernible.

"Jasmine."

eight

JASMINE?

She heard the word *Jasmine*.

Was it a name or was it a flower or tea?

Was he dreaming about buying her flowers, or making her tea?

Probably not. She wasn't born yesterday.

Was he dreaming of another woman?

Most likely, yes.

Liz closed her eyes and felt jealousy enter her blood. Her blood began to boil and she didn't like it.

Resentful over his past, a past he shared with *Jasmine*. Or could she still be in the picture? *Oh bother...*as she stood up from her loveseat to dump out her cold coffee. She had been romantically watching him sleep for the past hour and she was hot under the collar, so to speak. *Who was this Jasmine? Would Google know? YouTube?* He was a celebrity—there were bound to be photographs.

Liz ran to her iMac and did a Google search on *Jasmine Abbasi* and found nothing. Then she typed in *Tavas Abbasi girlfriend* and there she was...there they were.

A dozen or so girlfriends.

Blondes.

Brunettes.

Redheads.

He doesn't have a type. She could be any of these women, so she decided to search: allintext:-Jasmine-Tavas

And *viola*!

There she was...blonde hair and brown eyes...slender, tall and gorgeous.

Her Doppelgänger?

Except for the gorgeous part, she was just a younger version of herself. Photos of them walking, talking, unaware of the paparazzi taking pictures of them. Eating at restaurants, out in the park, dancing, kissing... one with them yelling at one another?

That photo peeked her interest, and she instantly clicked on the weblink associated with the image. It brought her to one of those TMZ type gossip sites that usually spew out half-truths. The column read:

"Lovebirds In Fight"

Lovebirds?

Liz rolled her eyes and read on:

> Jasmine Cornwall, Britain's top fashion model and Tavas Abbasi, America's internet mogul spare off in London's Granary Square. "The two were apparently arguing on whether they should change the color of their bridesmaids dresses," an insider reported. "They had a terrible row."

Liz nearly burst out laughing until she focused on his face. He appeared angry enough, she had not witnessed this side of him before, the couple must have had an argument about something. Miss Jasmine Cornwall appeared that she had been scolded and wasn't looking directly at him...*wait, bridesmaid dresses?*

He was engaged?!

Liz looked at the date of the article. *February 24, 2018,...* Three months old?

Not married—he told the truth. But she didn't ask the right questions. "Damn."

"That wasn't a very pleasant good afternoon, either," Tavas joked, as he brushed her shoulder with his fingertips and then accidentally glanced at what she was studying on her computer. "Well," he sighed, disappointed. "Here comes the twenty questions."

Liz smiled, "No, I have none."

Tavas circled his eyes around her face before he set towards her kitchen. "Coffee?"

Liz turned back towards her monitor, and eyed Jasmine Cornwall again. She was very photogenic, with her curly blonde hair and dark sunglasses. She had seen her photographs in magazines before, and Liz guessed he was right, she did have questions. "Here," she let go, getting up from her seat. "Let me make a pot so we can have a chat."

Tavas grinned into her brazen attitude, and then sat down on one of her bar stools at her kitchen island. He watched her make the coffee in silence, before he voiced, "Her name is Jasmine Cornwall."

Liz clicked on the coffee maker and then leaned up against her quartz countertops upset, "I Googled her."

Tavas laughed, then eyed Liz who was frowning. His smiled dropped, "What else did you Google?"

"I've just decided that I don't really care," Liz whipped out, banging and clanging the drawers and cabinets. "You and I have officially entered back into the platonic world. Business only going forward, understood?"

Tavas half-smiled then dropped his eyes to the coffee pot slowly percolating, "Can I ask you a personal question?"

Liz let out a huge sigh, then looked away for a second to swallow her pride. "Go ahead."

Tavas cocked his head to one side, "How old are you?"

Liz languidly closed her eyes. *There was that dreaded question she wished to avoid.* "Forty-five, my birthday is next month." *There, she admitted it. What she expected next was a goodbye, cya!*

Tavas scanned her posture and instantly felt her resentment. "My mother is forty-eight, you're only three years younger than she."

"Well, then, we'll have lots in common," Liz spewed, walking over to her upper cabinets and reaching for two coffee cups.

"Why are you upset?" He asked, sitting up straight.

"I'm not upset," Liz quipped, lifting up her chin.

"You're lying," Tavas said, shifting in the bar stool.

"No, I'm not," Liz said, indeed lying.

Tavas looked her up and down first before explaining, "I own a public company, Liz...but cherish my privacy. If you really want to know about my past, all you have to do is ask."

"I no longer want to know," she said, rolling her eyes.

"Are you jealous?"

Liz hadn't noticed it before but he had changed his clothes. When he walked in with AJ he had been wearing a nice white dress shirt and blazer. He was now wearing a black T-shirt and jeans. "Where did you get those clothes?"

"Your son's closet, I think we wear the same size," he teased, trying to reach behind his neck to look at the tag.

"Not funny," Liz uttered, frowning now.

"You're avoiding the question," he said, a little impishly.

Liz poured him and herself a cup of coffee. She handed him his, the creamer then sugar and stomped over to the other side of the kitchen. Sipping hers black, she voiced, "I'm not jealous. I just think you and I don't fit. Our age differences are too wide."

Tavas stirred the cream in his coffee, "I'm not bothered by our age difference, why are you?"

Liz closed her mouth, then took another sip, "You're as old as my son."

"By a few years."

"I'm old enough to be your mother," Liz quipped, rolling her eyes and gazing out towards her windows and vista.

"But I don't view you as being a woman of your age," he explained, becoming a little frustrated.

Liz noted it. "How do you view me?"

Tavas cocked his head, and then got off the bar stool. "When we first met, that day at the roulette table, I was so attracted to you. It overwhelmed me so much, I had to leave your presence."

Liz bit down on her lower lip, his admission lit a fire in her belly. "Why?"

Tavas licked his lips before confessing, "Because it made me weak in the knees."

She tried to disguise her smile by looking away from him.

"Then when we bumped into each other at the nightclub," he confessed, "...I knew it must be fate."

nine

LIZ AND TAVAS made love for the third time that day and lie naked entwined in each others arms. It was in the middle of the night, and the French doors were wide open with the ocean waves crashing down below them.

Tavas laid on his back and brought Liz into his chest. Kissing her on her shoulder first, he said, "We broke off our engagement."

Liz turned her head and looked up at her ceiling. "I didn't ask."

"But you were thinking about asking."

Liz laughed in her throat, "Maybe I thought about it."

"I knew it," he gushed, rubbing her thigh with his other hand.

"What happened?" Liz asked, bathing in his gentle touches.

"She had a change of heart."

Liz felt like she was pressing the issue, but she wanted no secrets between them. "Why?"

Tavas let go a sigh, "She didn't want to quit modeling."

Liz grew quiet for a second. "Why would she have to quit modeling?"

Tavas rolled over on his side and crunched a pillow under his head. Bringing the sheet up over their nakedness, he relayed, "Because I asked her to."

Liz sat up and held the sheet up over her breasts. "You asked her to quit her career?"

Tavas tried to pull her down. "Yes."

"Why?"

He now sat up himself, "Because I come from a traditional family where the spouse does not work."

Liz threw her head back in laughter, "These days?"

Tavas looked at her seriously, "Yes," he said quietly, "I am quite adamant about it."

Liz laid back down and stared up at her ceiling fan. Watching it turn around and around, she whispered, "You managed to surprise me again."

"How so?" Tavas asked, lying back down with her.

"You live in an age where technology can be developed by either a man or a woman, I'm living proof of that. Your livelihood is rooted in technology and you harbor a prehistoric attitude of women belonging at home."

Tavas closed his eyes. He wasn't going to budge, his belief was too deep-rooted. "I don't want to have a debate over this. Let me give you forewarning, you will not win."

Liz hooted this time and sat back up. "We're not debating, Tavas...I'm just giving you forewarning modern women won't agree to that."

Tavas laughed out loud now. "I beg to differ. I have thousands of letters from women all over the world willing to stay at home, run my household and raise my children."

Liz grew solemn and let his statement sink in. *Raise his children?* "This isn't gonna work. You're still so young, successful and you will want a family sooner than later. I'm *Miss Fun Right Now*."

Tavas threw his head back in pleasure, "*Miss Fun Right Now*, that's funny."

"Glad you think so," Liz quipped, swinging her legs over the bed. "But I've never been more serious."

Tavas quickly rolled over and grabbed Liz by the waist before she got off the bed, "Wait," he said, pulling her back down. "Can't we just live in the moment?" He then gave her a kiss on the lips. "Enjoy each other's company and see where this goes?"

"You want to keep seeing each other?" Liz asked, amazed.

Tavas circled his eyes around her face, "Of course, don't you?"

Liz looked deep into his eyes. She was in love with him, she's known so for quite some time. She would sacrifice her own happiness for his if she had to. She was just about to answer him when her phone rang. "Hold on," she said, as she leaned over to pick up the receiver. "Hello?"

"Liz?"

"Cass?"

"Liz, Rayna went into premature labor, she's at the hospital, come quick!"

A fear spread through her. "I'm on my way."

ten

CASSIE AND WYATT were already sitting in the waiting room. Eyes raised, every time someone either walked passed or got up from their seated position. Both on edge, nervous and anxious for some kind of news.

"She said she was on her way?" Wyatt asked, running his hands down his pant legs.

"Yes," Cassie quietly voiced. Biting down on her lower lip, she gazed around the area. The room was full when they first arrived, now there were only four people left, them and another couple. "She must have caught traffic on the freeway."

Wyatt nodded his head and then looked up to see Liz hurry in with a man. "There she is."

The twosome stood to their feet and went to greet Liz.

Liz ran into Cassie's open arms and hugged her tight, "Is she okay? Is the baby okay? What's happening?"

Cassie let go of her friend, and then replied, "She's in labor, she was bleeding and they tried to stop the blood. They wanted to do a C-section, but she said no."

"Tim is beside himself," Wyatt said next. "He was out here with us for about an hour then the nurses called for him to come into the delivery room."

Liz wiped away a tear before she asked, "How long has she been in labor?"

Cassie wiped away her own tears, and replied, "About two hours, the baby was in distress."

Liz covered up her mouth with her hand within hearing the grim news, and turned and fell into Tavas' arms. He held her tightly and raised his eyes and noted her friends quizzical looks. He released her quickly.

Tavas wiped away Liz' tears with his thumbs. "Your friends?"

Liz let go half a smile then turned around, "Oh shit—Cass, Wyatt, this is Tavas. Tavas Abbasi."

Cassie pulled in her smile and leaned over to shake Tavas' hand, "Nice to finally meet you."

Tavas shook her hand and then leaned over to shake Wyatt's. "Tavas Abbasi, nice to finally meet you as well."

The foursome whipped their heads around when Tim entered the room.

A hush overcame the area as they noticed Tim's eyes, red and swollen.

Liz closed her eyes, his dreaded look of despair was overwhelming.

Cassie covered her mouth up with her hand.

Wyatt spoke up for all of them, "How is she?"

Tim eyed everyone, including Tavas and explained quietly, "Rayna is fine."

A sigh of relief was heard through the small space. Cassie and Liz both wrapped their arms around one another's waist.

Tim continued, "It was stressful there for a while, she

lost a lot of blood. She was in and out of conscious and for a minute there, my heart stopped."

Cassie let go of Liz and then walked over to Tim to give him a hug, "But she's fine now? Is she awake, can we go in and see her?"

Tim gave Cassie a squeeze then said, "She's in recovery, they're cleaning her up—she had the C-section after all. But we can all go see the baby."

Cassie burst out crying, "What? What did she have?"

With tears in his own eyes, Tim answered, "A little girl. She's tiny though, about five pounds. The hospital put her in an incubator, but we can all still go see her they said."

"Oh my God!" Liz cried out in relief. "A girl? Rayna had a girl!" She turned to Tavas again who could feel the elation coming from her body. Reaching out for her again, they hug each other near in reassurance.

Tim leaned over and held out his hand to Tavas, "Tim Thompson...happy Daddy."

Tavas smiled and released Liz for the moment to shake Tim's hand, "Tavas Abbasi, boyfriend, congratulations."

Liz smiled inwardly and kissed Tavas on his lips. Together, they walked over to Cassie and Wyatt who were about to walk out of the waiting room. But first, Wyatt went into hug Tim to give him a congratulatory hug, then Cassie with a kiss on his cheek.

The five all walked down the corridor in silence, taking in the comfort that their best friend, wife and recently new mother was fine and out of danger. Reaching the glass to the nursery, Tim walked over to the nurses station and announced, "Tim Thompson, father. Can I hold my daughter?"

The nurse looked up at him and over at the anxious adults behind him. "Sure, Mr. Thompson, I will bring her to your wife's room in about five minutes?"

"Is she awake? Can we all go in now?"

"Family only," she cracked back.

"We *are* family," Cassie quickly replied.

"We're sisters," Liz added.

The nurse's eyes bounced from one woman to the next. Blonde hair—brunette—blue eyes to brown. "Yes," she said, gathering up some paperwork. "I can see the resemblance." She gave the women a big smile and then to Tim, she replied, "I'll bring her in."

Cassie and Liz both held hands as they reached Rayna's hospital room.

Tavas held back and announced, "I'll wait out here."

"You can come in too," Tim said, "this group is family. You'd better get used to it."

Tavas nodded his head, and then walked in behind the women with Wyatt.

Cassie and Liz stopped short of Rayna's hospital bed. Gazing at one another first, they watched Rayna as she slowly opened her eyes.

"Did you see her?" Rayna asked her friends, lifting her head up.

Cassie walked over to her friend's side, and leaned in to give Rayna a kiss on her cheek. "Not yet, they're rolling her in. Do we have a name yet?"

Liz walked over to Rayna's other side, and smoothed over her strawberry blonde hair before giving her a kiss as well on her forehead. "How ya feeling?"

"Like shit," Rayna quipped, trying to move her legs. "The anesthesia made my limbs numb."

"So you had the C-section?" Cassie asked, alarmed.

"Yes," Rayna admitted, "I had a difficult labor, then started to bleed."

Tim came over and reached in to give Rayna a kiss on her lips, "I love you so much, you did good babe, *real* good."

Rayna reached up and caressed her husband's cheek and in the corner of her eye, spotted the nurse rolling in their daughter. Perking up, she voiced, "Here she is...our little girl, our angel...our Myra Grace Thompson."

Cassie and Liz both started to cry again. *Myra* was Rayna's grandmother's name and *Grace* was Tim's mother's name. Both women passed away a year ago.

eleven

CASSIE HELD MYRA GRACE FIRST. Cradling the bundle within her arms, she gushed, "Oh my goodness, she is so pretty!"

Tavas concentrated on Cassie holding the newborn in her arms. He remembered seeing Cassie for the first time during his initial video chat with Liz. Cassie was a looker too, but in a diverse sort of way. With long brunette hair and bright blue eyes, he smiled at her presence and the babe within her arms. "You are a natural," he genuinely voiced. "You have children?"

"Yes," Cassie said, looking up at him hovering over her. "I have three kids, all grown now."

"Nice," Tavas said, "but the possibility for grandchildren."

Cassie peeked down at the baby again, "Yes, I never thought of that before, but yes. I would love to be a grandmother one day."

Liz stood behind them and heard their conversation. Tavas was so enthralled at the potential of becoming a parent one day, and she hated knowing she could break his heart. She could never give him children. Her period ended last year, entering early menopause at forty-five. The doctor told her that since she started her period early on in life, she recalled at the age of nine, then early menopause was a possibility. "My turn," she expressed, holding out her arms.

Cassie stood up and then handed her friend the baby. "She's so precious."

Liz cradled her in her arms and sat down on a nearby chair. "She sure is."

Tavas sat down next to her and touched her shoulder with his hand. "She's beautiful."

Liz looked up at him and then back down at the baby, "She is. Oh, and she has Rayna's light red hair!"

Tavas gently lifted the babies hospital cap and eyed the strawberry blonde hair. "What a sweet little angel."

Rayna gazed over at Liz sitting next to Tavas and noted their closeness. She turned to look at Cassie and called her over. "How long has this been going on?" She whispered in her ear.

Cassie gazed over at the two and whispered back, "A week, I think."

Liz looked up from the baby, "I can hear you."

Cassie started to smile, "So how long?"

Tavas lifted his head from the baby for a second, "A month."

Liz gazed at Tavas then back at the girls. "A month," she confirmed, smiling.

"What sort of accent is that? What nationality are you?" Wyatt asked, sitting next to Tim.

Tavas noticed that everyone except for Liz looked his way. "I was born in Tehran."

"Oh," Wyatt replied, "I had a business partner once who was from Tehran. It's nice there."

"You've been?" Tavas asked, interested.

"Twice, actually," Wyatt said, sort of matter-of-factly.

Cassie raised her eyebrow, "I never knew that."

"Now she knows," Wyatt laughed.

"Where in Tehran?" Tavas asked Wyatt not testing him, but generally interested in getting to know everyone better.

"We stayed in Ekbatan?" Wyatt explained to everyone. "We were there with my friend's family to watch a soccer—*football*—game in Azadi Stadium."

"Nice," Tavas let go, "you like soccer?"

"Love soccer, you?"

"I love league ball, you watch league?" Tavas asked, excited.

"Professional soccer, the Galaxy mostly," Wyatt announced.

"I'd like Liz to someday accompany me back to Tehran, but I don't see her ever leaving the safety of her beach."

Liz met his eyes and gave him a sneer, "Not true," she explained, looking down at the baby again. "I've been to Maui, three times."

"Another beach," Tavas grinned into her.

Everyone laughed.

"Good luck getting her out of that house, Tavas," Rayna uttered, sipping her ice chips. "Liz only leaves her house for food."

"We met in Vegas, no?" He asked around at everyone.

"Special occasions and *food*," Cassie added, snickering.

"And the occasional purse," Liz smiled down to Myra Grace.

Cassie started to hoot, "Oh, watch out for her, have you seen her special closet full of handbags? She's obsessed."

"Not obsessed," Liz protested, then she met Tavas' eyes. "Maybe just a little."

"You look so comfortable holding her within your arms," Tavas whispered to her.

Liz smiled inwardly and looked down sad. *How was she ever going to tell him? She could never give him children.* Liz bit down on her lower lip, and replied, "I always wanted a little girl."

"You can babysit every other date night," Rayna let go, holding Tim's hand in hers. Tim got up and sat on the edge of Rayna's bed.

Liz laughed, then the baby started to whimper. "I think she may be hungry," she proclaimed, walking the baby over to hand her off to Rayna.

With open arms, Rayna took her little one and began to open up her gown.

Everyone turned their heads to give her natural privacy and Rayna pulled up the bedsheet and covered their view of her breast and nipple in the babies mouth.

Tavas was especially enthralled with mother and child, and his eyes were fixated on the act.

Cassie noticed his study, and asked, "How many kids do you want?"

"At least three," Tavas admitted without thinking.

At that moment, Liz tilted her head and bore into Cassie's eyes.

twelve

LIZ AND TAVAS parted ways at the hospital. By the time they got out of the building it had already been the afternoon of the next day. Tavas was expected to be at a social media conference, and had to head out and catch a plane to Texas.

Liz wanted to drop everything to join him but she too had responsibilities of her own.

But the moment they parted ways, Liz felt apprehensive.

She had never been in a relationship before where there were so many obstacles. She was older, he was younger, she lived in California, he lived in Colorado. He was famous, she was an introvert. He wanted children...she could no longer have them. Could love conquer all? Liz was not so sure anymore.

Liz was glad that Cassie could come by and spend the day with her shopping. They were at The Beverly Center in Beverly Hills and the two girls did some purse hunting.

"When are you gonna tell him?" Cassie asked, wandering about.

"Tell him what?" Liz said, searching the shops and trying to ignore the obvious.

"That you can't have anymore children," Cassie reminded her.

"Soon," Liz remarked. "Very soon."

"Oh, look at this one," Cassie exerted, pointing to the leather bag.

Liz took a peek at it, "I want red."

"Not into white anymore?"

"No, not really," Liz let go, eyeballing multiple bags.

"This one?" Cassie asked, holding the red purse up for her to view.

Liz shook her head, *No.* "Let's go to Carmela's, that boutique usually has bags there I love," she said, walking away.

"When is soon?" Cassie yelled at her backside.

"Soon!" Liz yelled up in the air.

The girls head out of the boutique and walk towards the mall square to walk among the crowds of shoppers. Liz wasn't paying attention in particular when her eyes rested on people waiting in line at a book signing. She couldn't see who the author was from her angle, but definitely could read the name on the marquee...

Aaron Tobin
The Falcon Prince

Liz stopped cold. Aaron had literally hundreds of people standing in line at his book signing. *Another book,* she thought. *Her ex-husband wrote another friggen book.*

Cassie stopped cold, and then looked in the direction that Liz was staring. "Oh, you've got to be kidding me. What are you gonna do?"

"Nothing," Liz plainly said, beginning to walk away.

Cassie started to walk with her when she noticed the line splitting apart. "I think he's taking a break."

"So," Liz proclaimed, looking straight ahead.

"Don't you wanna congratulate him?" Cassie asked, turning to look back at the crowd.

"Not really," Liz uttered, looking around for Carmela's. "There it is."

Cassie turned her head and bumped right smack into someone trying to get around her.

Aaron Tobin?

"Cassie?" he asked, excited to see her.

Cassie smiled, then opened up her arms for him to walk into. "Aaron, how are you?"

Aaron then stiffened up when he grabbed hold of his ex's scowl. "Elizabeth."

"Aaron," she quickly spat out. Cassie felt uncomfortable and decided to put an end to the cold greetings. "You wrote another book?"

Aaron turned away from Liz and then unconsciously spurted out, "Yea, my wife encouraged me to write another."

Liz now concentrated on just him. With sandy brown hair, glasses over blue eyes and a goatee, Aaron Tobin appeared average to her now and she would have never be interested in him again. *Wife. He said, wife. He got remarried?* "When did you remarry?"

Aaron grinned at Liz' olive branch, and then honestly admitted, "Six years ago."

Six years?! They were barely divorced six years. Asshole. "You piece of shit," Liz let go angry. "You were seeing her when we were married, weren't you? You two were having an affair?"

"Elizabeth," Aaron calmly voiced, "not here."

"Don't call me that," she angrily snapped back. Then she started to laugh. "Not here, not there, not now, not then." She then adjusted her purse on her shoulder in annoyance. "You know what? I don't care anymore. It no longer matters," she said, starting to walk away when she heard her ex confess...

"The boys have a brother."

thirteen

IT HAD BEEN a few days since she seen or heard from Tavas. He had sent her an email with his itinerary as an attachment (LOL) that he was heading to New York on business next. His return flight was yesterday and she still hadn't seen or spoken to him.

Should she worry? Not really. She trusted him and couldn't wait to tell him about everything that happened in the past few days.

Her ex had shocked her with both his admissions. He had been married for six years and his son was also six. Aaron told her later, after Liz had calmed down that his wife, Veronica was pregnant when they signed the divorce papers.

He looked really happy, and she was happy for him. She told him she had finally found someone who completed her and Aaron was happy for her. They said their goodbye's and walked away from him and it gave her closure. The truth and real reason their marriage had failed.

Liz' heart began to pound when a video chat icon popped up on her iMac. Clicking it excitedly, she beamed when she saw his face. He appeared healthy, rested.

"Hi," she let go elated to see him.

"Sorry I couldn't reach out sooner, we had an incident here at the studio that I don't want to talk about, but will when I see you."

"And when is that exactly?" She asked with a pout.

"Miss me?"

"Terribly," she admitted, rolling her eyes and sighing.

"How much?" He asked, with a seductive grin.

Liz unbuttoned her blouse and then bared her neck down to her pink bra to tease him. "This much."

She was then surprised and concerned when the camera went black.

Her doorbell rang and her heart dropped. She ran to the door, opened it and jumped into his arms.

He barely got through the door and swung her body around, kissing her everywhere.

They crash down together onto the floor and on top of her great room rug. Tavas continued to kiss her high and low, her eyes, her lips, her neck, her throat, her breasts until he broke away and asked, "Is anyone else home?"

Liz lustfully said, "No, just me."

"You will do," he revealed, trying to pull her shirt up over her head. Anxious and impatient, he tugged at her gym pants and was unable to pull them down. "Take these off," he demanded, "take everything off, I want you naked *now*."

"Do you want to go to the bedroom?" She asked, adjusting her weight underneath his body.

"No," he honestly admitted, "I don't think I can wait that long."

"Love your impatience," she voiced, kissing his neck and tasting his skin. Liz then discarded all her clothes and laid there naked on her white fuzzy great room rug. Extending her arms up over her head, she reached out to feel the softness of the rug underneath her fingertips.

Tavas pulled the rest of his clothes off, and laid down between her legs. Now that she was finally naked, the urgency was no longer apparent. He took his time to caress every inch of her body, all the while kissing her open lips and chin.

Tilting her head back, Liz allowed him to buss his lips across her neck, down her throat, and around her ears then finally resting on her breasts and nipples. Suckling, licking and nibbling as she ran her fingers through his thick head of hair.

Bucking her hips for him to cross the threshold, Tavas obliged and entered her by slow degrees, watching her face as he steadily filled her.

Eyes open, he relished in the glow of her anticipation of reaching the end. He pumped and moved his hips to and fro, up and down and held her body close all the while kissing and getting off on her pleasure.

fourteen

LIZ AND TAVAS sat down on the sand in a cove and watched the sun set. With their arms wrapped around one another, they let the ambiance soak in.

Liz was truly happy. She hadn't recalled when the last time she felt complete or satisfied with life. She could tell that Tavas too, was blissfully happy and the two of them soaked in the twilight and after effects of their lovemaking minutes before.

"Will you fly back with me to Colorado? I want you to see my studio, stay at my home."

"You know I don't even know where you live? I mean, I know you're in Colorado because your invoices say Lake City, CO."

Tavas laughed and then gazed out towards the surf, "That's where I live Lake City, over Lake San Cristobal. I can't wait for you to see my view. Do you need to fill out a vacation request for your boss?"

Liz smiled at his humor, "Ha-ha." Then she grew quiet and thought about it. *Why not? She hadn't been on vacation in over seven years! It was true, she was a workaholic. Getting up to work without brushing her teeth or pouring herself a cup of coffee. She was a recluse, preferring to stay indoors to being out. She was even shocked he got her outside and sitting on the sand!* She leaned into his shoulder and squeezed him tight, "I will go with you."

"Terrific," he said, excited. "I will call my pilot and announce we have another passenger."

"Your pilot?" She asked, amazed.

"My pilot, his name is John. He used to fly jets over Afghanistan, now he flies for me."

Liz looked at him oddly, "You mean you have your own plane?"

Tavas gave her a sweet kiss, "I love your innocence sometimes, Liz—I have a Learjet."

"What?!"

* * *

Stepping off the plane wasn't as incredulous as where they landed. Everything surrounding the airport was so *green*.

Tavas noted her bizarre look, and replied, "I like the seasons. I love the snow."

For some odd reason, Liz got excited about the idea of seeing and being in snow too. "I haven't been to the snow since I was little. When does it snow here?"

"I give it two more months," Tavas plainly replied. He held her hand as they walked through the airport, and while he made a phone call on his cell she heard him say, "Bring the car out front," then hung up the phone.

Liz was astonished to see a black Mercedes Benz waiting for him to pick them up. He held the door open for her as she got inside.

Soaking in all the nuances, Liz smiled inwardly...*she could get used to this.*

En route to the studio, Liz was in awe of her surroundings, she was used to high scale decor, palm trees and outrageous homes and scenery, but Lake City and its majestic mountains were another world. With their small town mom and pop shops, log homes and country laid back feel.

"Now you know why I live here," he told her, getting out of the car and taking her hand again to lead her out.

They arrived at a large red brick building. "Is this your studio?" She asked, gazing up at the few stories.

Tavas shook his head. "Yes, I can't wait for you to meet my team. Everyone is local, and if I need specialists, they either telecommute, or do what you do, fly in for the day."

They barely made their way through the reception area when a woman stepped into Tavas and blocked his way in. He stood immobile and silenced, and stared straight into her eyes.

Liz stopped walking and noticed he dropped her hand at the sight of her. And what a sight she was…Liz recognized her immediately—Jasmine Cornwall, ex-fiancee, there to create some havoc.

"Mr. Abbasi," the receptionist relayed, "I apologize, but Ms. Cornwall asked to wait for you in the lobby."

Tavas waved her off, "No need to apologize Mindy, I got this." He then turned to Liz and gave her half a smile. "I have to deal with this, it shouldn't take too long." He turned to Mindy now, and stated, "Mindy, can you please show Ms. Tobin to our talent seating area?"

"Sure thing, Mr. Abbasi."

Liz was taken to a large comfy room with lounge chairs, ottomans and love seats, a refreshment table and water bottles galore.

She sat down on one of the loveseats and gazed down at her watch. *Yes, she was going to time this little unscheduled visit. Why was she here? Why now? After several months of not seeing one another, why would she want to see him now? What could he have to say to her? She broke it off with him, didn't she? Ohmigod, she thought. What if she changed her mind? What if she was there to get him to change hers? What if she was...pregnant?*

Liz was about to run on a tangent when she gazed down at her watch. *15 minutes....* She got up frustrated and went to get herself a water bottle. Twisting off the top, she tipped it up so she could pour the water down her throat. She made a quick turn of the room, and began to wander aimlessly when she looked down at her watch again. *30 minutes...* She was just about to open up the door and walk out to go look for Tavas, when the door opened, and in stepped her worst nightmare.

Ms. Jasmine Cornwall, high fashion model in from Britain in all her voguish glory.

She stood a few inches taller than Liz, but then again, she was wearing heels; Liz was not. But the blonde hair was the same, even the eyes. And in those eyes she felt her pain and wondered what was said and why she came to look for her.

"You're Liz, right?" Jasmine asked, exposing her pearly whites.

Liz dropped her eyes to her smile, and wondered how much those veneers cost as well. "Yes, why?"

Jasmine languidly walked in and leaned her tight butt up against the side of a loveseat. "I just flew in to give him back his ring."

Liz blinked back her surprise. "His ring?"

Jasmine let go another brilliant smile, "Oh, he didn't tell you about the ring?"

Liz collected herself, and then reeled in her jealousy. "No, he didn't."

fifteen

LIZ LOOKED at her oddly and noted she was irate. "Where's Tavas?"

"He's talking to his production manager," she let go taking out a cigarette from within her purse, and lighting it. "He was due on a tape, and he missed his cue."

Liz watched her puff on her cigarette then search for an ashtray. Discarding the tip of it in an empty paper cup, she looked across at Liz. "Where did you two meet?"

Liz looked at Jasmine and was no longer threatened by her presence. She appeared lost for some reason. Misplaced and a jumbled mess. Liz casually walked over to the couch across from her and sat down. "Sit down Jasmine, I'm not the enemy."

Jasmine smiled, then took another puff, "Thank God for that."

Liz smiled then watched her take a seat. "How long does taping usually take?"

"About an hour," she coughed, "not very long."

"We met in Vegas," Liz relayed, smiling and taking a sip of her water.

"Oh, at a convention?" Jasmine asked, taking another puff and blowing out the smoke at the side of her mouth.

"No, at a nightclub," Liz honestly confessed.

Jasmine hesitated for a moment and eyed Liz up and down. "You're so his type."

Liz nodded her head, "Hope so."

"You're a little older than he likes, but his *type*."

Liz could tell she was trying to bait her. But she wasn't going to take that troll. "I could tell straight away that he was into mature women."

"That's typical," she let go, chuckling.

Jasmine smiled, and then pointed her finger at her, "I like you."

"I'm a likable person," Liz let go, congenial.

Jasmine chuckled, "You remind me of my mother."

Liz tilted her head, "Oh yeah?"

Jasmine nodded her head and then looked down at the ground, "She died a few years ago from cancer."

Liz grew increasingly sympathetic towards her. She wanted to hate her but she just couldn't. Jasmine couldn't have been more than twenty, twenty-one, and her compassion for her morphed into some kind of parental desire to shelter her from harm. "I'm sorry for your loss."

"Thank you," Jasmine genuinely said, taking another puff. "She never wore much makeup either...I miss her terribly."

Liz stood back and watched her face fill with suffering.

"I still have feelings for him," she said, sadly, "that hasn't gone away." She then gazed down at her fingernails and spread them out admiring her new manicure. "But I don't want to quit just yet. My career has just started, ya know?"

Liz nodded her head.

Jasmine continued, "I've worked to bloody hard to get this far. And now I'm being offered film roles," she explained with her British accent.

"I get it," Liz spoke out, "you've followed your dreams. No one can fault you for that."

Jasmine nodded her head too. "It's a sacrifice, I know," she continued on, "something I feel I might regret in the end but I feel so passionately about succeeding."

Liz noticed the tears in her eyes and got up and walked over to her. Extending her arms out for her to walk into, Jasmine didn't hesitate and stepped into the embrace.

Liz gave her a maternal hug and rubbed her back to comfort her. She was just about to whisper some comforting words when in the corner of her eye, spotted Tavas entering through the doorway.

"What's this?" He asked the girls, hugging one another.

Liz let Jasmine go and watched her body show embarrassment. "Just showing concern."

"She's a keeper Tavas," Jasmine let go wiping away a tear.

"I thought you left," he said to Jasmine, walking over to be by Liz' side.

"Just needed a fag," she reacted, taking her last puff and then snuffing it out in the empty cup. "I knew you allowed cigarette's in the talent area…and I wanted to meet your new girlfriend."

"Now you've met her," he said, relentless.

Jasmine smiled towards Liz. Extending her hand out for Liz to shake, she voiced, "Yes I have. Take good care of him."

Liz looked deep into her eyes, "I plan to."

Jasmine tipped her head *farewell* and left through the door.

Tavas closed his eyes and then stayed quiet until Jasmine was out of sight. He turned to Liz and then took a step backwards. He anticipated fury but didn't receive any. "You OK? Is the coast clear?"

Liz grinned, and then wrapped her arms around his neck, "You're mine, right?"

"Right," he said, leaning in to brush his lips across hers.

"Then what is there to be jealous about?"

Tavas welcomed the maturity in their relationship. "You're really not jealous?"

"Why…should I be?"

"Not at all…It's *over* between us…it's been over for a while," he said, dropping to his knees.

Liz' eyes grew wide, "What are you doing?" Then she watched Tavas pull out the black velour box that Jasmine just returned, that housed his mother's four carat diamond ring. Taking it out of the enclosure, he took Liz' hand.

"Will you marry me?"

sixteen

TOO FAST.

Really too fast.

What was she going to do?!

Flying back from Lake City felt odd to her. Normally, she would be excited about coming home, taking off her bra and sitting down at her computer. Walking through her door however, she felt incomplete and lonely.

Tavas had proposed to her and she felt nothing but confusion. Even though she had the best time while she was in Colorado, the fantasy burst the moment she stepped back onto that Learjet.

She left Tavas with no definitive answer. Not a *yes* but not a *no* either…it was a *maybe*…and she was sure when she decided on that, but now she was in total doubt.

The loneliness was thick in her isolated house. Looking around at all her pristine furniture, freshly cleaned floors and immaculate kitchen, she had never felt more single. She had been living by herself, working by herself for so long, she forgot what it felt like to be a couple, a team.

Tavas was a little sad, she could tell so straight away. He got up from his knees and looked solemnly down at the ground. Like someone had just sucker-punched him in the gut, he was speechless. What was he going to do? Beg her? She was glad he didn't and said nothing afterwords, until he kissed her goodbye at the airport.

"You'll think about it?" He asked, his two arms still around her in an embrace.

Liz closed her eyes and relished in his warmth, "Yes, Tavas, I will…"

Liz wandered around her kitchen intending on making herself some oatmeal when she heard her doorbell ring.

It couldn't have been Tavas, she thought. The plane couldn't have made that round trip in under an hour.

Liz put down the oatmeal mixture and headed towards her door. Through the peephole, she wondered who it was and was taken-back when she saw Dave Edelburg on her porch.

What the heck could he want?

She hadn't seen Dave in a very long time. Liz opened up the door and smiled at him as he smiled back.

"Hi, how are you?"

Liz tilted her head to one side, "Good, how are you?"

"Good," he voiced, gazing around her front yard. "I see you took out the rose bushes."

Liz dropped her eyes to the African Daisies she planted last year. "The raccoons were eating the buds and I never really got to enjoy the flowers."

Dave laughed and then dug his hands down his jacket pockets. "Are you busy? Have I caught you at a bad time?"

Liz hesitated and looked him up and down. Dave Edelburg was the one who got away. If not for him reconciling with his wife, she would have married him without a doubt. A few inches taller than Liz, Dave had dark brown hair, brown eyes and a gruffly look about him. He was also very smart and she recalled how she used to love to hear him talk. Very articulate, and well mannered. She opened up the door and watched him walk right in like he owned the place.

Taking a few steps in the great room, he discarded his jacket on one of the chairs and his eyes instantly targeted her vista of the water beyond. Walking over towards the balcony, he stopped short of the French doors. "I missed this view," he softly said, looking right then left.

Liz stood her ground. He wasn't there for a social call, that's for sure. *So what the heck did he want?* "So Dave, I haven't seen or heard from you in over a year, what's going on?"

Dave unlatched the door and opened it up. "Can we go outside and talk? You know I've always loved the sea air."

Liz walked behind him as he made his way onto the redwood. She sat herself down on one of her outdoor couches and then asked, "Why are you here?"

Dave gave her half a smile and then sat down himself. "I want to apologize for my behavior."

Liz cajoled, "You could have emailed me. My Gmail hasn't changed."

Dave accepted that retort. "What I'm trying to say Liz, is that I'm sorry...I know I hurt you."

Liz bit down on her lip. That was the truth. Their breakup was painful and it took her this long to free herself from that discomfort. "You did hurt me Dave."

"I know," he continued, leaning forward, stopping short of touching her. "I know, I'm sorry."

Liz shook her head. "I accept your apology."

"Thanks babe—"

"Don't call me that," she snapped at him, shifting her body oddly on the couch.

Dave leaned back and gazed out towards the beach, "I'm sorry, it was a habit."

"A habit you had sixteen months to get over," she reminded him.

"Has it really been sixteen months? A year and a half?"

Liz nodded her head, *Yes*. "So, what have you been doing? How's work?"

"I closed that Benjamin deal, you know the one I included your help on?" He plainly said, eyeing some seagulls flying up above them. "Closed a few more after that, for a few months, I was in high demand."

"That's good, I'm happy for you," Liz quipped, gazing up at the seagulls as well. The birds were interested in some crabs making their way out of the surf and onto the sand. "How's your wife?"

Dave grew quiet for a second then looked down at his shoes, "She had cancer, Liz."

Liz swallowed her mirth, "Cancer?"

"She was diagnosed two years ago, and lost her battle last month."

Liz looked deep into his eyes. *This was the reason he came to see her. To reach out for comfort...*she could tell he needed someone, his body was itching to lunge for her. "I'm sorry to hear that Dave, I didn't know."

"I haven't been working lately, can't concentrate on business," he said, sort of matter-of-factly.

"That's understandable."

Dave then sprung forward and fell at her knees. Wrapping his arms around her midriff, he laid his head on her lap. "I miss you Liz. I miss us."

Liz felt compelled to show him compassion but her hands screamed revolt. But the past swarmed her reason, and she laid her hands on top of his head and hair. Smoothing his hair through her fingertips, she softly voiced, "I used to miss you, Dave. So much in fact, I used to cry myself to sleep."

With his head still in her lap, he uttered, "She had cancer, Liz. I felt guilty for leaving her and the children. She needed me."

"I needed you too," Liz quipped in return.

"I *know*, I'm sorry," he voiced, lifting up his head and then pushing up on her body to kiss her.

Liz wanted to receive his kiss, but shifted her head away. "Don't."

Still in her lap, he voiced, "I want to kiss you so badly Liz."

Liz shook her head. It was all she ever wanted at one point, to have a second chance with him. She would have given anything back just to be by his side. But *now*...she realized what she was supposed to do and her role going forward in life. "But I don't want to kiss you."

Dave was surprised at her reaction, and took it for playing hard to get, and for *no* really meaning *yes*. "I miss you."

Liz pushed his body away and then stood up to her feet. "I met someone," she said, looking him in the eye. "In fact, I'm in love with him, Dave. He asked me to marry him..."

seventeen

TAVAS SHOWED UP AT LIZ' door. Instead of crashing down to the carpet like they did the last time, Liz held him off and asked him to sit down. She decided to keep Dave's visit a secret for now. No need to mention an event that no longer matters. What mattered now was her revelation.

Tavas preferred to sit outside in the sun so they both headed out onto the balcony.

Thank God for her balcony...

Liz had to tell him before they got married that she could no longer have any more children. That a dream of his would never be fulfilled if he married her. It would be a test...

Tavas sat down in shock after Liz' confession.

Liz started to tear up knowing that Tavas would be hurt from her declaration. "I'm sorry," she ended up saying, trying to ease his pain. "I know how much you want children."

Tavas stood up from her side and ambled over to the balcony's edge.

Liz' heart nearly broke in two at the sight of him contemplating his next move. She sat silent and confused about his silence. She watched his backside as he just stared out at the blue horizon. "Tavas?" She asked, gently.

He barely turned around, "Ya-ya," he expressed, shrugging her off.

Liz bit down on her lower lip, and wiped away tears that had fallen down the side of her cheeks. Swallowing her next words, she didn't want to push the issue. She knew deep down that he was struggling with the idea of never being a parent.

Tavas caused her to jump when he turned around quickly. "How long have you known this? When you and I have been together countless times, making love without protection, and not once did you tell me that you couldn't have children?"

He was irate, she could tell so now. She had never experienced this side of him before. She was glad to see and feel his passion. Even his face altered. *Did he want to retract his proposal?* She was no longer sure about anything. "No one is to blame here, Tavas. Our relationship has been casual until now. I didn't feel the need to divulge that fact, not until your proposal...and maybe when I saw you with Myra Grace at the hospital."

"Even then you could have told me!" He yelled out, frustrated with the subject.

Liz took a step backwards, she expected some kind of reaction, but not like this, she had to try to calm him down. "There will always be a better time—and we could go on for hours playing the *what-if* game, but the truth is—I'm being straightforward with you *now*."

"You're just like Jasmine!" He shouted back at her. "If I wanted to go through life with no children, then I could have just married her!"

And just like that, Liz and her maturity level flew right off the balcony and she shouted back, "Fine! Then, why don't you just go back to her! I'm sure she will gladly take you back."

Tavas walked to the other side of the balcony. He gazed down at the steep ledge and thought about jumping over. "I don't want *her*—I wanted *you*."

Liz' heart leaped for joy—it was a positive sign. "You can still have me. I love you Tavas, more so than any other man. You complete me, challenge me, finish me, love me like no other. You're my soulmate, and I don't want to lose you."

Tavas gazed away and broke down. Bending over to his knees, he let out a terrible wail, which caused Liz to run over to be by his side.

They came together at once hugging and embracing one another with a fierce passion no one else could come between.

Pulling close to her ear, he cried, "You won't lose me. I love you Liz. I am your soul's mate, I've known so since the day I saw you. I love you with all that I am."

Liz reached over and kissed his neck, "I love you too, Tavas, I would do anything for you—you must realize that."

Tavas leaned away with his arms still around her, "Even sell your home and move to Colorado to be with me?"

Liz wiped away her tears then lightly kissed him on his lips, "Even sell my house and move to Colorado."

Tavas sighed then kissed her lips softly, pulling languidly away he asked, "Even sacrificing seeing your friends every week?"

Liz closed her mouth. *She never once thought about that...*

eighteen

IT WOULD BE A HARD TEST. Saying and doing are too different actions. *Yes*, she confessed, *she would do anything for him*—would that include leaving her friends?

It's true it was just across state, her friends could easily drive or catch a plane to come out and visit her or vice versa. And her boys, both in college now, adults, with lives of their own, they could also come to visit when on a break from class, summer vacation or holiday.

What else was tying her down? Why was it such a hard decision to make? To rattle her comfort, her routine, the places and people she had come to count on and appreciate. Didn't she just rattle his world as well? Thinking he would someday become a parent, only to find out his natural choice was never an option if he were to marry her.

She should be happy, but she felt sick, afflicted with change and discomfort and now doubted her decision to marry him.

She looked on her life thus far. Clear and precise, acknowledged her life lessons, and learned from them. There would be many changes involved with this proposal and she was sure she could meet those adjustments.

Grabbing his hand, she led him back to the house and down to her bedroom. Standing just short of her door, she quietly voiced, "Even not seeing my friends for a while." She bent forward and ran her hands up his chest and kissed him.

Tavas responded to her touch immediately and cradled her face with both hands. Opening her mouth up with his tongue, he kissed her deeply with warmth and adoration. Liz wrapped her arms around his backside and with one hand, pulled his shirt up and caressed his heated body.

She loved him, she thought and realized instantly, *was deeply in love with him.*

Tavas picked up her body, kicked the door closed behind them and laid her down softly on the bed.

Tearing down her bra, he cupped one breast and bent down and engulfed her flesh, kneading and sucking, while Liz ran her fingers through his hair and admired her priceless emerald cut diamond ring. It was an heirloom, passed down from generation to generation, so much devotion was behind this ring. Tavas released his mouth and hands to unbutton her jeans to liberate her of the remainder of her clothes.

Naked now, Tavas widened her legs and buried his face and mouth between the crux, softly licking at her clit and delving his tongue lightly inside, in and out around and around.

Liz reached down and grabbed his hands back and placed them up over her breasts and shouted out her orgasm in sweet delight to his ears.

Barely having time to breathe, he turned her body over, opened up her legs from behind, lifted up her hips and quickly entered her, painlessly pumping and jolting up and down up and down until his seed spilled and repeated euphoria.

Still lying on her stomach, Liz could feel his fingers gently caressing her buttocks and the softness of her arch. Languidly moving his hips up and down, Liz could still feel his fullness deep inside her. She could get used to this part, and looked forward to many more nights in his bed.

nineteen

LIZ WOULD HAVE to overturn her entire life, step out of her comfort zone, and walk toward potential happiness.

She finally found the love of her life. Yes, he was younger than herself, but mature enough to know better and necessary to learn from experience and take good advice.

She admired his work ethic and what he was able to accomplish at twenty-nine. Driven and focused, he wasn't a devil may care entrepreneur who foolishly spent his millions on extravagances, but instead invested his money wisely and showed gain and purpose, and she thought Dave was her ideal! Being a CIO of a highly sought after software programming company, Dave was an amateur compared to Tavas' expertise.

Liz later learned that along with his YouTube Channel and video podcast, Tavas also conducted seminars and offered them across the United States and Europe. He ran an annual membership database with over fifty-million paid subscribers and managed a staff as CEO for over 300 employees across the states. He maintained thriving offices in both New York and London and was a personal investor who owned stock in several major high profile companies. He was known throughout the Silicon Valley as an angel investor to hundreds of startup companies, many of which were sold to Google, Apple and IBM.

Tavas Abbasi, to her, was the ultimate prize, and if he weren't already a handsome man, she would have fallen in love with his brain. He was a metro-sexual, who dressed in the finest clothes, quality leather loafers and wore the most expensive colognes. He smelled good, he tasted divine ,and she loved the way he simply looked at her!

She would have gladly bore him ten children if not for her age for she knew he was her *Albert* to her *Victoria*.

She was head over heels for the man and couldn't wait to be with him always.

"I'm not going to sell my house like I originally planned," Liz explained to Tavas over video chat.

"Why?" He asked, looking down at some paperwork.

Liz sipped on her Starbucks frappuccino, then continued, "I think it's more sensible to rent it out."

"Oh," Tavas said, now looking up to her face.

"I spoke to a real estate agent and she said I could get more than five to seven grand a month for rent in this neighborhood. And," she stopped to sip, "with my unsurpassed view of the ocean, I could possibly ask for ten grand."

Tavas smiled, "I like that number."

Liz smiled back, "Me too."

Liz turned to Cassie and Rayna, thank goodness for girlfriends! They met Rayna at her house in Santa Clarita. The baby had finally come home from the hospital and the girls couldn't wait to be altogether again.

Rayna had been breast-feeding in a rocking chair, while Cassie and Liz both got comfy in a nearby loveseat. The three girls were in Rayna's new nursery built especially for her friends and family who came to visit.

Cassie and Liz were both sipping coffee, when Cassie spoke up from the moment of silence. "Isn't it funny how in a span of twelve months our lives have all changed?"

Rayna gazed up from the babies feeding, "I know what you mean."

"Right?" Cassie asked Liz, watching her eyes zoomed in on the baby. "How I had been searching for a relationship online and met no one until Wyatt spilled that bucket of water at the school?"

Liz nodded her head in agreement, "I know, and now you've sold your home and moved to Ojai to live at Wyatt's ranch with his daughter Jennifer and Kendra."

Rayna gazed down at Myra Grace and noticed she had fallen asleep while feeding. She unlatched her mouth from her breast, and then held her little body up to her shoulder to gently pat on her back to release any gas bubbles. "I think my life has changed the most," she let go, whispering.

Cassie raised her eyes and smiled, "Most definitely."

Liz took a sip before saying, "I totally agree."

Rayna now began to rock back and forth in the rocking chair. "Letting go of my past," she softly voiced, continuing to rub the baby's back and shoulders. "Allowing friendship to alter into commitment. Trusting in love enough to let love come to me. Myra Grace changed my life for the better."

Liz now contemplated the huge change in her own life, and regarded the life-changing decisions her friends both have made. She loved Tavas and she knew he loved her. "Tavas has asked me to marry him."

Cassie bit down on her lower lip, "I would shriek with excitement, but I don't want to wake the baby. And your answer?"

"I said yes," Liz graciously smiled.

Cassie then reached over and gave Liz a hug, "I'm so happy for you."

Liz gave her friend a squeeze, "Thank you so much."

Cassie reached out and grabbed at her hand, "And everything is okay? No reservations?"

Liz gazed over at Rayna first then confessed, "None, whatsoever."

Rayna now spoke up, "I knew it, I fuckin' knew it."

Liz laughed, "How so?"

Rayna gazed down at Myra Grace first before saying, "When I first saw him walk into my hospital room after I had the baby, I thought to myself, how nice he was to come with you to make sure you were okay."

Liz gazed down at the fluffy pink pastel rugs on the floor. "He was attentive, wasn't he?"

Cassie smiled graciously, "He fit right in."

Liz agreed with her, "He did, didn't he?"

"Like he was always part of our group," Rayna added.

"Just like Wyatt and Tim," Cassie acknowledged and grinned.

twenty

LOVE IS A COMPROMISE, love is a challenge... love tests your devotion.

Working from home means working from *anywhere*. She was just trading a sunny beach view for a wintry mountaintop.

Tavas grew up wanting a spouse to stay at home, now he had one, but with one little difference, his wife *worked* from home. He also wanted children, with one little compromise, now he gives his guidance to *millions* of children who need his expertise.

* * *

Liz and Tavas were married on the beach below her home. Liz wore a very tight, slimming beige gown, while Tavas wore a black T-shirt, black blazer and bare feet.

The wedding reception was also held on top of her balcony overlooking her gorgeous vista as a last hooray, and was intimate except for the celebrity photographer on hand releasing digital photography of their happy union to his website, YouTube channel and various media outlets.

It was her second week of marriage, and Liz finally moved in all her belongings from her Malibu home into Tavas' hillside home in Lake City, CO. Moving most of her heavy furnishings into storage, Liz held a consignment sale for the small home goods and gave the rest to charity.

Tavas promised her a honeymoon the moment he returned from Japan, and asked her to pick a destination anywhere on the planet. *Wow...anywhere?*

Where should she go on her honeymoon? Just let your imagination wander...

Lake City was a sleepy little town with down-home folks and the last time Liz was at his estate, she had already saw the living room, den, kitchen, bar area, media room, formal dining room, the disco, billiard room, study, library, game room, wine cellar, pantry, butler's area, sitting and powder rooms, and, of course, his bedroom. But Liz was never able to investigate the 'west wing' of his property. The East wing was where Tavas did most of his living while the West had been saved for guests and for his mother when she came to visit.

His mother was given an extravagant guest suite with master living area with ensuite bathroom. His mother liked that part of the house because she was able to play her piano in quiet, and was able to hear the melodies echo down the corridor.

Unpacking the rest of her boxes could wait, right now, Liz felt like exploring her new domain...

Liz wandered down the hallway and peeked in every room. Picture perfect spaces with furniture right out of a magazine. Walking into one room in particular, Liz noted the furniture and surrounding area was in her taste.

White Country?

Liz ambled in further and admired everything around the living area. Watercolored photographs on the walls, pastel floral arrangements, and barn wood adorned smooth white couches and loveseats.

Liz thought it odd for a second that Tavas—or maybe his interior designer—had the same taste as she, until white double sliding barn doors called out her name. She stood immobile for a second, then sprung forward to spread out the doors.

So many feelings passed through her body in that moment: amazement, awe and elation, until she burst out in tears. So much emotion swelled inside her as she brought her hand up to cover her mouth.

Liz walked in and around her new home office.

Impeccable.

Unique.

Feminine.

With every updated technology readily available to humankind: desk phone, copy and fax machine, laminator, solar cell phone charger, laser printer, iPad tablet, dozens of tester mobile phones, wifi scanner, paper shredder, eReaders, docking station, postage meter and even a mounted wide screen TV. In the corner was a personal kitchen with sink, refrigerator and her own coffee maker.

A gorgeous farmhouse desk made of recycled wood held up her iMac, file folders, desk accessories and their wedding photo with additional photographs of her best friends Cassie, Wyatt, Rayna and Tim, while an ergonomic chair in creamy beige was there for her to sit in.

In the corner of the room was a gorgeous antique hearth with wood burning fireplace, and in a sitting chair beside it were two purses: a red Louis Vuitton, and a pink crocodile Gucci.

And, without a doubt, the best thing about her new home office, were the floor to wall windows with a 190° view of the wintry covered mountains, the white tipped Pine and Douglas fur trees, smoke coming from the chimney's beyond, the blue-black lake…and the majestic falling snow.

about trisha

Hey, it's Trish...

I'm a Romance Author of 34+ books, plus an Indie Book Publisher of 48+ Pen Name Authors.

I've been writing romance with a whole lot of heat lately. I love to write fun, fast romances with witty leading ladies getting that gorgeous, sexy, yet lovable guy that doesn't take months to finish. Happily Ever After with a little bit of love angst in between. Whether you yearn for Historical or Modern, I always have a story for you!

Rejoice, Romance Reader...

For upcoming releases, book news, and other goodies, subscribe to my Newsletter!
https://mailchi.mp/567874a61a56/aab-landing-page

- instagram.com/authortrish
- amazon.com/Trisha-Fuentes/e/B002BME1MI
- facebook.com/booksbyTrish
- youtube.com/theardentartist

also by trisha fuentes

❋ **Modern Romance** ❋

A Sacrifice Play

Faded Dreams

Never Say Forever

* * *

❋ **Historical** ❋

The Anzan Heir

Magnet & Steele

The Relentless Rogue

One Starry Night

In The Moonlight With You

Captivating the Captain

The Merry Widow

Unrequited Love

The Summer Romance of the Duke

✻ Series ✻

HOLLINGER

Dare To Love - Book 1

A Matchless Match - Book 2

Arrogance & Conceit - Book 3

Impropriety - Book 4

SERVICE•DAUGHTER

The Steward's Daughter - Book 1

The Cook's Daughter - Book 2

The Curator's Daughter - Book 3

THUNDERBOLT

The Surprise Heir - Book 1

A Dance of Deception - Book 2

Win the Heart of a Duchess - Book 3

OBSESSION

Unsuitable Obsession - Part One

Broken Obsession - Part Two

ESCAPE

Swept Away - Book 1

Fire & Rescue - Book 2

The Domain King - Book 3

A G E • G A P • R O M A N C E

Whispers of Yesterday - Book 1

His Encore, Her Ecstasy - Book 2

Against the Wind - Book 3

www.ingramcontent.com/pod-product-compliance
Lightning Source LLC
LaVergne TN
LVHW051951060526
838201LV00059B/3597